DUTCH
PUBLISHERS

Illustrations Nicolas Trottier
Text Martijn de Rooi

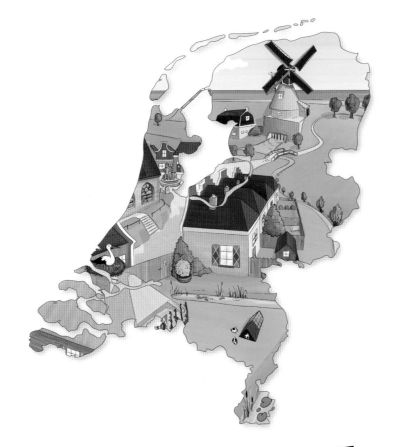

Hans Brinker

A classic Dutch adventure

Hans Brinker is a real Dutch boy. He lives with his father, mother and sister Greetje in a village close to the sea. The family's house lies just outside the village, near the dunes and the beach.

In the summer, Hans and Greetje often play on the beach. They like building sandcastles.

And sometimes Hans scares his sister by picking up a crab!

Hans' father is a lock keeper. He operates the lock in the canal next to their house. The water on one side of the lock is higher than on the other side. This looks really strange. Hans' father makes sure that boats coming from the sea arrive safely in the canal to continue their journey.

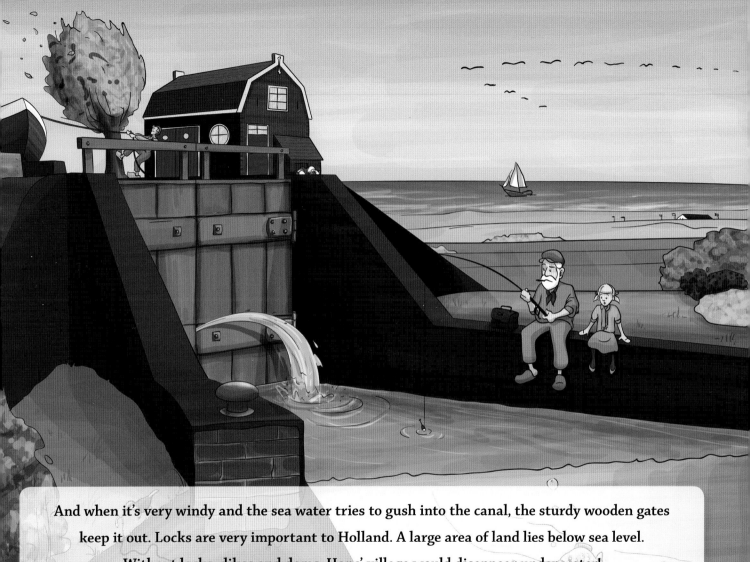

And when it's very windy and the sea water tries to gush into the canal, the sturdy wooden gates keep it out. Locks are very important to Holland. A large area of land lies below sea level. Without locks, dikes and dams, Hans' village would disappear under water!

In the winter, it is often so cold that the waterways are covered in a thick layer of ice.
Whenever this happens, Hans and Greetje go ice-skating with their friends. Hans loves doing this.
He often races against his friends; who will be first to reach the windmill? Hans does his best to win,
but this doesn't always happen. When the children are cold, they go and eat pea soup at the stall
next to the windmill. This really warms you up.

Hans rides his bike to school. The school is in the village and a long ride away, but Hans doesn't mind this at all. He cycles along the dike and listens to the birds singing their happy songs.

Sometimes a rabbit runs alongside him. In the summer, there are beautiful flowers growing on the slope of the dike. When Hans cycles home, he sometimes stops to pick some of these flowers for his mother.

One day, Hans is cycling back home in a happy mood. Suddenly, he realises that it's getting cold and dark. Grey clouds start to gather as the sun disappears. Hans feels slightly uneasy and decides to cycle a bit faster. But then his eye catches something! He can see a trickle of water coming through a hole in the dike! Hans knows straight away that this is a dangerous situation. A small hole can soon become a big hole and then the village would be in danger of flooding!

Without a second thought, Hans leaps into action. He jumps off his bike, clambers up the dike and sticks his finger into the hole. Phew! The hole is closed. The water stops coming through the dike. But what now?

Hans is standing there all alone. Night is falling and it's starting to rain harder and harder. Hans is becoming very cold. He sees how the animals go in search of shelter. But he can't leave, because otherwise...

Hans calls for help, but no one can hear him. He thinks about home, about his mother and father who are bound to be worried. And about his sister Greetje, who is now tucked up warm in bed.

Early in the morning, farm hand Gerben is cycling along the dike. He is on his way to work at the farm.

He is startled to see Hans. 'What are you doing here, Hans?' he calls out. 'The sun hasn't even risen yet!'

Hans is happy to see somebody at last. 'Go and fetch help, quick!' he shouts. 'There's a hole in the dike and I'm keeping the water out with my finger, but I can't keep this up much longer. We have to save the village!'

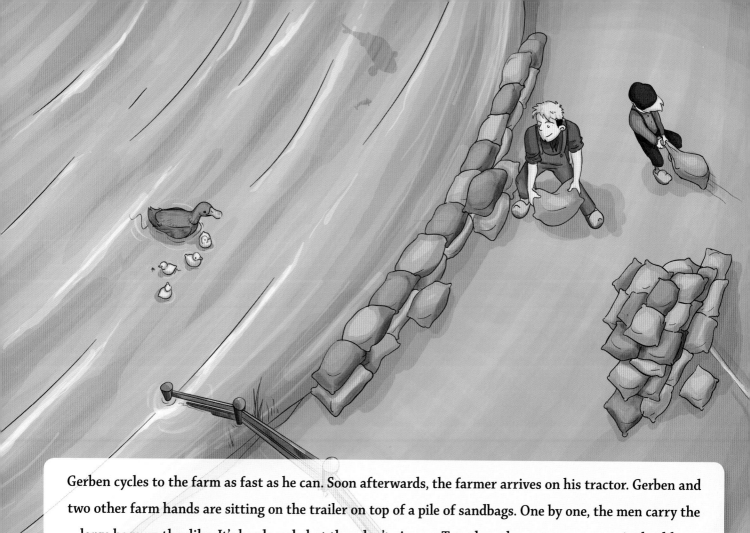

Gerben cycles to the farm as fast as he can. Soon afterwards, the farmer arrives on his tractor. Gerben and two other farm hands are sitting on the trailer on top of a pile of sandbags. One by one, the men carry the large bags up the dike. It's hard work, but they don't give up. Together, they manage to repair the dike. They've done it! The hole is plugged and the village has been saved!

The farmer places Hans on the front of his tractor and they drive to the village.

Once there, the farmer tells the mayor all about Hans' efforts to save the village from flooding.

Soon enough, the whole village hears about what has happened. The villagers hang out flags and rush outside to applaud Hans. It turns into a huge party and Hans is honoured as the village hero!

21

Suddenly, Hans realises that his mother is standing next to him. She smiles at him and kisses his head.

Hans yawns and stretches out his arms. He isn't quite awake yet. This is clear to see.

'Did you sleep well, Hans?' his mother asks him while opening the curtains. Hans looks around sleepily.

'I did, but I had a very exciting dream. And I'm still a bit tired, too.'

Colophon

Hans Brinker
A classic Dutch adventure

Published by Dutch Publishers
Publishers Allard de Rooi, Wilbert Collet
Illustrations and graphic design Nicolas Trottier
Text Martijn de Rooi
Translation Tekom Vertalers, Hoofddorp, the Netherlands
Printing Scholma Druk, Bedum, the Netherlands
Thanks to Ronald de Niet, Francine Siemer-Ankersmit

ISBN/EAN 978-90-76214-13-9
First printing July 2009

Trade distribution Nilsson & Lamm bv, P.O. Box 195, 1380 AD Weesp, the Netherlands
Telephone: 0294 494 949. E-mail: info@nilsson-lamm.nl
Business-to-business www.dutchshop.nl

Dutch Publishers, Dutch Image and **Dutchshop** are registered trade names of **The Ad Agency**
P.O. Box 340, 2400 AH Alphen aan den Rijn, the Netherlands
Telephone: 0172 449 333. Fax: 0172 495 846
Internet: www.theadagency.nl. E-mail: info@theadagency.nl

Also available in Dutch
Ook verkrijgbaar als Nederlandstalige uitgave
ISBN/EAN 978-90-76214-12-2

More books about Holland can be found on **www.dutchshop.nl**

Game

Find the right page number for each drawing.